Phil

The only thing that could keep up
with little Phil Groundhog was . . .

. . . his shadow!

No matter how fast he ran . . .

HOGZILLA
. . . or how high
he jumped,
his shadow
followed his
every move.

Whether he laughed . . .
HOGZILLA
HOGZILLA
. . . or cried,
his shadow
was always right
there beside him.

Even when Phil
felt small . . .
KONG
GYM

. . . his shadow
could make
him feel
bigger.
♫ Pretty hippos out walkin' with gorillas down my street! ♫
KONG
GYM

But everyone grows up.

Even groundhogs and their shadows.

Grown-up groundhogs
are expected to act
a certain way.

But Phil's shadow
had other plans.

Phil's idea of the perfect vacation was taking the bus to the local beach.

Shadow dreamed of visiting faraway places.

Phil loved scary movies. Shadow, not so much.

Phil enjoyed eating dandelions, clover, and tree bark.

Shadow craved something spicy.

Phil liked to be on time.
Shadow liked to stop and smell the roses.

At first Phil found Shadow's behavior amusing . . .

. . . but a little off-key.

Phil's friends
found it amazing . . .

. . . and a little . . .

. . . gross.

But soon it got annoying . . .
Give Roses
Give Love
Phil

. . . and then downright embarrassing.
P.U.!

Phil had
had enough.
Why can't you be like other shadows?

I wish you would just go away!
Phil

But then he thought about it.

Phil said he should go away.

And he had always wanted to travel.

So that night . . .

. . . and the next morning . . .

. . . and a couple of days later . . .

. . . and into the following week . . .
. . . that's exactly what he did.

Back at home, Phil tried everything to find his shadow.

He posted signs.

LOST

HAVE YOU SEEN MY SHADOW?
IF FOUND,
KEEP SHADOW OUT OF
SHADE AND CALL
555-5555
IMMEDIATELY.

He used the newspaper.

GROUNDHOG SEEKS SHADOW

Fun-loving homebody groundhog is looking for lost shadow. Please come back, Shadow, so we can hibernate together. I promise things will be different.

SKUNK

Then he saw Shadow making news . . .

Suddenly Phil's life seemed pretty dull. He longed to be exploring with Shadow.

Halfway around the world, Shadow realized something was missing. He had no one to share in his adventures.

The thought of searching
for Shadow scared
Phil silly.
He'd have to travel
far and wide.

But the next morning . . .

USS PUNXSUTAWNEY
. . . and a couple of days later . . .

. . . and into the following week . . .
. . . that's exactly what he did.

He searched . . .
Shadow?

Shadow?
Shadow?
Shadow?

. . . and
searched . . .
Shadow?

. . . and searched some more.

Finally, when he could search
no longer, he had an idea.

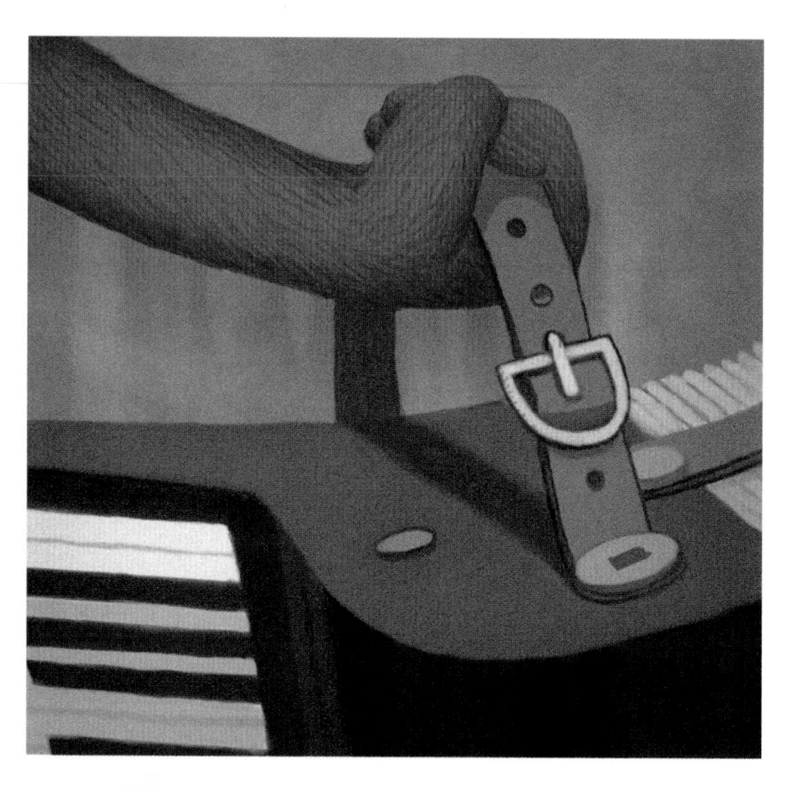

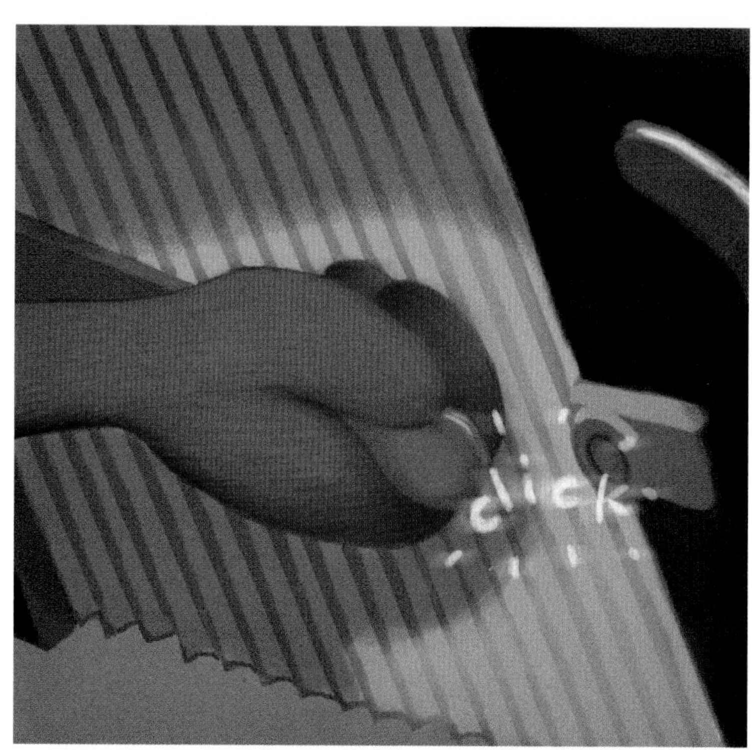

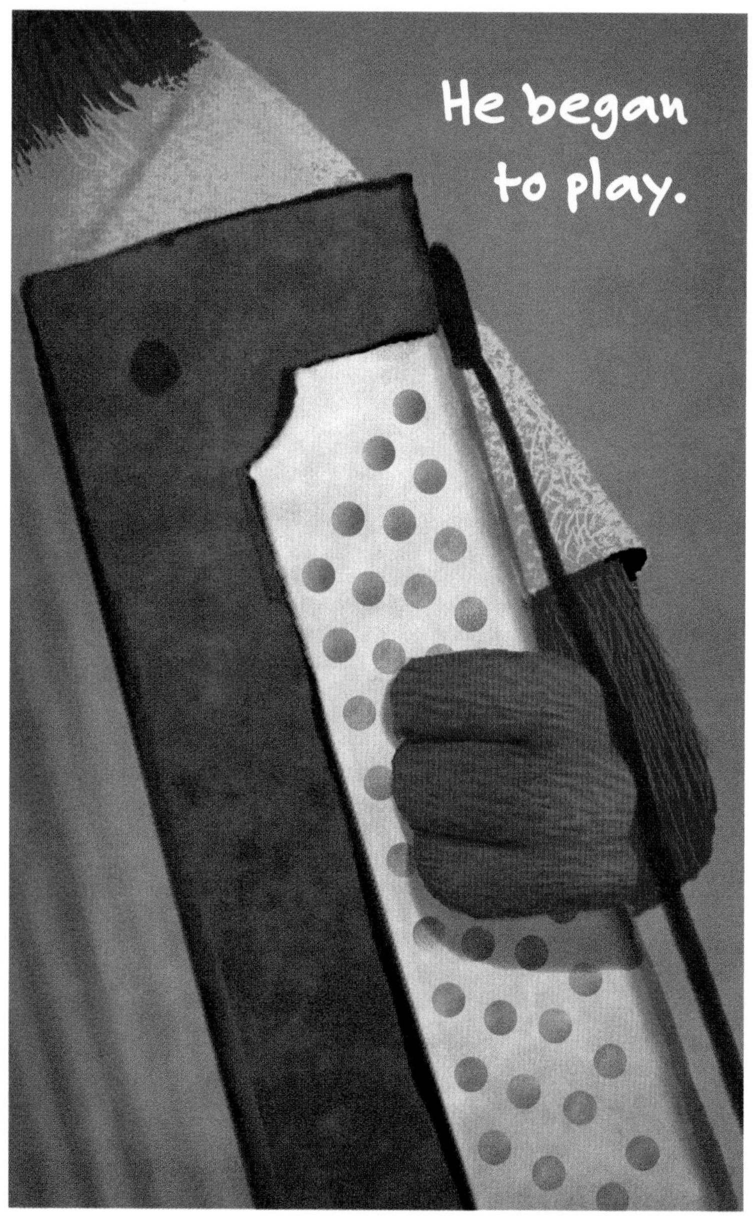

He began to play.

And when
he did . . .

. . . he heard
someone . . .

. . . gently
accompanying him.

The two friends played together,
this time in perfect harmony.

And the next morning,
and a couple of
days later,
and forever after,
that's exactly
what they did.

To Justin, Alec, and Julia, whose shadows never stray.
Special thanks to the amazing Nicholas Rivera.

Published by Charlesbridge
85 Main Street
Watertown, MA 02472
(617) 926-0329
www.charlesbridge.com

Illustrations done in Adobe Photoshop
Hand lettering by Julia Biedrzycki
Text type set in Felt Tip Bold by Mark Simonson
Color separations by Colourscan Print Co Pte Ltd, Singapore
Printed by 1010 Printing International Limited in Huizhou, Guangdong, China
Production supervision by Brian G. Walker
Designed by Diane M. Earley

Library of Congress Cataloging-in-Publication Data
Names: Biedrzycki, David, author, illustrator.
Title: Groundhog's Runaway Shadow / David Biedrzycki.
Description: Watertown, MA : Charlesbridge, [2016] | Summary: Little Phil Groundhog and his shadow do everything together, but when they grow up the more adventurous shadow wants to travel, so he leaves—but neither is happy, so Phil goes searching for his friend.
Identifiers: LCCN 2016013770 (print) | LCCN 2016015128 (ebook) | ISBN 9781580897341 (reinforced for library use) | ISBN 9781607348948 (ebook) | ISBN 9781607348955 (ebook pdf)
Subjects: LCSH: Woodchuck—Juvenile fiction. | Shades and shadows—Juvenile fiction. | Friendship—Juvenile fiction. | CYAC: Woodchuck—Fiction. | Shadows—Fiction. | Friendship—Fiction.
Classification: LCC PZ7.B4745 Gr 2016 (print) | LCC PZ7.B4745 (ebook) | DDC [E]—dc23
LC record available at https://lccn.loc.gov/2016013770

Printed in China
(hc) 10 9 8 7 6 5 4 3 2 1